THE GALLERY:
An Allegorical Journey

THE GALLERY:
AN ALLEGORICAL JOURNEY
A Ride into Life Novella

MINDY SAVOIA

XULON PRESS

Xulon Press
2301 Lucien Way #415
Maitland, FL 32751
407.339.4217
www.xulonpress.com

© 2021 by Mindy Savoia

All rights reserved solely by the author. The author guarantees all contents are original and do not infringe upon the legal rights of any other person or work. No part of this book may be reproduced in any form without the permission of the author. The views expressed in this book are not necessarily those of the publisher.

Any reflection or similarity to any story or person, fictional, living, or deceased is purely coincidental.

Unless otherwise indicated, Scripture quotations taken from the Revised Standard Version (RSV). Copyright © 1946, 1952, and 1971 the Division of Christian Education of the National Council of the Churches of Christ in the United States of America. Used by permission. All rights reserved.

Paperback ISBN-13: 978-1-6628-0694-0
eBook ISBN-13: 978-1-6628-0695-7

DEDICATION

To the memory of Anna, especially during those lovely times when we would sit and discuss this book over coffee.

ACKNOWLEDGMENTS

Steve, your love, support, and wonderful, creative ideas are gifts.

Pam, Michael, and Gabe, your wisdom and
guidance far surpass your years.

Nicole, you are appreciated for more than just wrapping up the title!

Jane, you are the anointed editor!

To my God, whom I praise and bless!

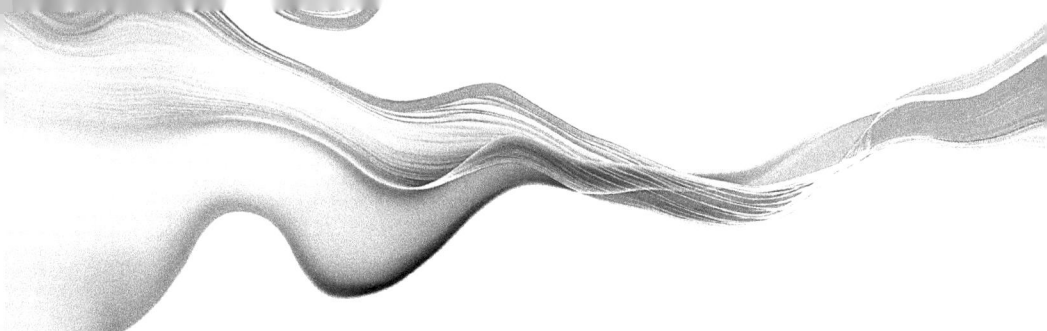

CONTENTS

Introduction xi

PART I – ARRIVAL

Chapter 1... 3

Chapter 2... 9

Chapter 3... 13

Chapter 4... 17

Chapter 5... 20

Chapter 6... 23

PART II – DESCENT

Chapter 7... 29

Chapter 8... 33

Chapter 9... 37

Chapter 10.. 40

Chapter 11.. 45

Chapter 12.. 49

PART III – ILLUMINATION

Chapter 13...56

Chapter 14...61

Chapter 15...65

Chapter 16...70

Chapter 17...76

PART IV – GLORY

Chapter 18...83

Bibliography 89

INTRODUCTION

This project began on a west bound flight back to Arizona, home to our immediate family since 1996. The images flooded my head, and I was compelled to transpose them through a keyboard. I always traveled with a laptop to keep up with work even during vacations. Being an administrator of a K-12 school filled my days, nights, weekends, and holidays. The year was 2012. Time moved quickly, spanning eighty-five to ninety-hour work weeks. *The Gallery: An Allegorical Journey*, often took a proverbial backseat, but God did not. Balancing family life, church ministry, and work was not easy with intense dedication to each. Spring of 2018 marked the season to initiate a personal life change.

We need to be aware of the ways God speaks to us and be ready to receive His word. The Lord's gentle nudging pushed me to reflect about retirement after enjoying a variety of employment settings that culminated in dedicating twenty years to one particular school, having been there from its inception. Consideration and prayer progressed into discernment, which led to the surrender of what my heart had recognized. Once the official state retirement forms had been put into place and my replacement found, the message was stronger than ever, "I have work for you." It was the familiar, quiet voice in the way He speaks into one's spirit.

The Lord's ways are not our ways, and He worked a completely new novel into my heart. *Ride into Life* became a Christian romance that was soon followed by its sequel, *Ride into Life: The Legacy – A Continued Journey* of *Love, Faith, and Healing*. While developing the background and construction of those first two books, the Holy Spirit led me to tie *The Gallery* into that series but position it as the third volume, portrayed through an atemporal setting.

Thus, the new journey of edging this book toward publication had begun. In fact, many paths in life commence and then continue with the focus on the process being as crucial as the final product. Often, the sequences do not neatly adhere to a green, amber, red, green light progression but rather a series of starts, stops, detours, races, and yields. *The Gallery* is meant to be an allegorical expedition through the scope of one's existence. It could potentially take place during or even after an individual's trek through natural life, thus making the work timeless in its application and meaning for the reader. God provides us with numerous opportunities to reflect on what He has given to us and how we use and build upon our earthly as well as spiritual resources while we nurture our relationship with Him. Is there one final judgment for each of us, or does life provide continuous possibilities to work on becoming closer and closer to the person we are meant to be?

Obviously, we do not have control over every aspect of our lives. However, our behaviors and responses to life's twists and turns are part of who we are and how we choose to be. Allow Grayson, a main character in *The Gallery*, to take you along on his journey. There may be parts of yourself you see in this person that you like, dislike, or are even afraid to face. Grayson's encounter with the Creator is his choice. His ultimate decision is his own, not God's. Our Lord offers direction while providing free will.

Readers of *Ride into Life* and its sequel, *Ride into Life: The Legacy*, will find a thread that connects the first two books' protagonist to Grayson, thus infusing further purpose to all three novels. Questions with real-life application, found at the end of each chapter of this work, are meant to present ideas to deepen a reader's understanding on many levels. *The Gallery* may also be utilized as a stand-alone religious piece for an individual or a group in a book study. It is my hope that in sharing this story, one can contemplate their own direction, and invite others to take part in a unique and personal experience with our Redeemer.

PART I
ARRIVAL

CHAPTER One

The steel grey hearse wheeled past as the procession of vehicles steadily followed, headlights glued to the next car in line. A matching vehicle, following the one with the deceased and filled with the obligatory funeral sprays, was second in the lineup. Tinted windows kept the passengers as well as onlookers at a respectful distance. The extended motorcade wound through the city streets, held together by the presence of police vehicles and a striking contour of limousines only associated with the loss of someone very important.

Dressed in a dark suit, Grayson stepped out from the sidewalk and into what appeared to be a fine mist as the rain came to an end. Clouds formed and seemed to meet the street, yet the temperature was neither cold nor hot. Grayson could see the curb and a portion of the lane in front of him as he walked. The path looked slightly illuminated, as if the sun was either beginning to shine through the haze or another system of cloud cover approached. The man continued on his path. There was no sense of urgency, yet he walked with purpose. Difficult as it was to navigate through the fog, I am sure, he thought, this is the way to go. Grayson walked on through the city.

Arriving at the steps of the building, Grayson took note of the vintage bricks and stonework that shrouded the edifice. The windows were framed with a lighter color stone than that which wrapped the exterior, starting just below the roofline. Paned glass filled each window with white trim into which every piece had been snugly fit. Marbled columns framed the front of the structure. One could certainly marvel at the architecture and handiwork of the builders so long ago. Those who put their effort into such labors must have been genuinely rewarded; perhaps the monetary compensation was not as great as the fulfillment of working on such a project. After all, was it not what the construction of this great country had been all about, Grayson nodded to himself?

The air seemed to clear a bit as steps came into view. The man walked up; he did not take hold of the brass handrails that had been cemented into the stone. Each piece was seamlessly fitted to the next. One could not tell where the mortar lines were located. As he ascended, the entrance came into view. A burnished brass plate, darker than the railings, affixed to the forward-facing wall, simply stated that this was indeed the entrance to the museum. The doors were heavy but moved with an unmatched evenness, considering the size, weight, and apparent age of the large hinges. Grayson expected that such a large, old door should certainly creak. The maintenance crew must be worthy, he mused.

He entered the building. Grayson made his way to a desk where an elderly gentleman in a uniform handed him a ticket. "That way," said the man as he motioned with his hand and a dip of the head. The staircase was finished with smooth stone. The bannisters, once again, were brass. There were signs to various rooms in the museum: "Ancient Cultures," "Natural History," and "Gallery," were a few that Grayson noticed.

"Hmm, Gallery," he quietly said aloud. As Grayson followed signs, he felt a sense of determination. The hallway leading into that part of the museum was not long. Walls were white and pleasantly lit. Simple frames dotted the walls and dividers, giving the impression that there was space enough for additional artwork. Who decides what is recognized, mulled Grayson? The curator must have to answer to someone; work is like that, he thought. One wakes daily and moves into the grind, never knowing exactly what will be encountered, even curators, Grayson acknowledged to himself. What pressures might such a custodian come across? What would he or she ultimately agree to in order to get the job done? One usually did not start a position with excessive yielding; it just happened—a means to an end. If a man acquiesced that much at the beginning of his career, he'd never make it to such a place of high status, Grayson justified to himself. Status and power, second only to material recompense, made the world go 'round. The physical world took care of the physical world. Grayson had no doubt about that.

As he walked along, Grayson admired the simplicity of the design, entering another corridor of art. These were not the Monets, Rembrandts, or van Goghs studied during the university days of his education. One might contemplate how new artists received the acclaim and recognition to be displayed within a revered institution. The intricacies of such creations stirred something in him. He never considered himself to be modeled after "The Thinker," but he was known throughout his community for stoic self-preservation.

When he was a child, his father would take him to museums. "Grayson," he would begin, "this is classic art. The sculptures have lasted far longer than those who knew the sculptor." And Grayson, as a child in a child's mind and body, would ponder on what it might be like to be carved out of stone, forever encased, never moving, breathing, running, playing, laughing.

Both parents believed in a firm foundation, although where his mother and father saw eye to eye did not include her emphasis on religious preparation and training; Grayson was more like his father on that note. His father, a man of impeccable stature both inside and out, was someone who could lead, and others easily followed. When Grayson's mother passed away at an early age, he remembered waiting and then wishing for his father to show some kind of emotion. There were no tears, noticeable depression, or angst. Life for the rest of the family simply went on, quietly and uneventfully.

Grayson observed and matured. He never remembered deciding to be the sort of person he became. There was school, attending church with his mother and siblings, and later, work, courtship, marriage, children, and a hint of retirement. He'd have time to decide about retirement—there was always time to decide. If only the marriage, well, marriages, had worked out. Who needed that anyway, he recounted? Plenty were always waiting, willing.

Mixed media—now that appealed to Grayson. Moving past the next divider, he admired how lines of paint blended with charcoal and spattered dyes, often intermingling wood and textiles woven into one another. What started as plant-based and then took twists and turns in careful development, had once again become melded as one. Was appreciation of art nothing more than perception or did it require actual in-depth presence? Was it about the lighting, colors, and textures? Did it require years of study? Would the inspiration of amateur talent ever end up within these heavily respected walls? To each his own, he thought.

Grayson looked up, suddenly wondering where the beautifully crafted windows were that he had admired from their exterior. He actually wondered if the panes were painted the same both inside and out. The man retraced his steps and concluded that he must have been within some inner chambers of the museum, since there were no windows to be found. Oddly enough, he did not remember passing any windows upon entering the great foyer where he was handed his ticket, which he estimated to have been over an hour ago. How long had he actually been there? Grayson absently glanced toward his watch and then repeated the action. Had he forgotten to put it on that morning? Now that was odd. The only occasion when he did not wear the timepiece, over his forty-plus years of owning it, was when he was once, briefly hospitalized.

Around the corner, there were still no windows, yet a blend of what may have been acrylics, called out to him. Silhouetted by indirect lighting, hung a vertical and narrow painting of a boy, framed with simple wood and a single matte. The background was rather generic. The foreground boasted an unclaimed carved, wooden toy train engine at the base of the baggy overalls, adjacent to a partially hidden striped and small, star-speckled rubber ball. A field of grasses spread over rolling hills in the distance. Dark hair and eyes appeared to have been created using an artistic technique that resulted in the appearance of a different grain from the rest of the canvas. The eyes beckoned Grayson to come closer. The disheveled hair was not as much unkempt as poorly cut. Maybe the lad couldn't hold still long enough to get the job done well, contemplated Grayson. He recollected a time, when he was just a boy of six or seven, sitting in a kitchen chair while his mother tried telling him stories and humming short tunes as she clipped the wisps of his unruly hair, smiling, "Got to finish before Father gets home, Gray-Bear." Mama always smiled when she called him that. She had a way of smoothing everything—his hair, his temper, his father.

When he started school, Mama walked him to the door, smoothed his hair and clothes, then blew him a kiss, whispering, "Gray-Bear." She was always there when he and his two younger siblings came home from school. She'd have food prepared and would cheerfully remind them, "No snacks until you change out of your school clothes and into your play clothes." She did that every day until … well, until she didn't any longer.

As Grayson peered into the boy's eyes, he wondered what his own eyes must have said in those younger days. What did they show now, as an adult? Who would notice? Who could see? A man of the cloth once remarked that there were no secrets hidden by the eyes. Grayson never believed that. A person shows what he wants to show, no excuses. We are all accountable for ourselves, good and bad, he reminded himself. He wondered whether the artist used a model; the painted boy's eyes were expressive, yes. Certainly, there was a sad knowing and slightly mischievous look. It might be interesting if an artist could capture the thoughts of a child in his eyes and then return to the same model and revisit those same eyes, years later, Grayson pondered.

Grayson glanced back at the painting before changing direction—"Hmm …" he could have sworn there was a ball at the boy's feet in the portrait.

QUESTIONS AND REFLECTIONS:

Do you feel that the physical world takes care of the physical world, as Grayson shares? What are the implications of your response?

What part(s) of a museum could you relate to as relevant to your life?

CHAPTER
Two

A field of late summer wildflowers carpeted the floor of the frameless watercolor. A bi-plane, superimposed above, was surrounded by an azure sky spotted with sparse grey-white clouds. Did the artist intend to have control over his or her palette? Watercolors, thought Grayson, often looked as if they had been fashioned by brushed strokes of freedom. One could imagine the pilot sitting in an open cockpit, created by simply blending a few wisps of color. The work was inviting and instantly stirred memories.

Grayson stepped onto the plane. His first flight was a solo voyage. Grayson's father had walked him to the steps of the aircraft, and shaking his son's hand, slipped him a twenty-dollar bill, just in case. "Your grandparents will meet you, Son. Listen to them and do as they say. Mind your manners and complete your chores before they ask. I'll see you the week before school starts." Grayson nodded. That was their typical father-son conversation.

That being his twelfth summer, it also turned out to be Grayson's best summer. The Midwest was a place a young boy could have some independence. Early mornings on the farm, long hot afternoons exploring, and never-ending evenings where skies darkened much too late dictated his freedom. Grandmother was not at all like the fading memories of Mama. She was, in fact, Father's mother. Her strict ways were more than an upbringing; they were the way. However, there was an underlying genuinely caring nature about the woman. She and Grandfather would go out onto the porch after the dinner dishes were washed, dried, and put away. They'd often invite Grayson to sit with them, inquiring about school, the rest of the family, and whether they still attended church, regularly. At least the boring burden of that obligation died with Mama. Next summer, it would be Annabeth's turn to visit and Thomas' after that.

It was Grayson's place to chart new territory. This was neither intimidating nor exciting; it was simply the way of the first born. Annabeth was not only the middle child, but a girl and the only female left in the home after Mother passed, while Thomas, who was the youngest, played baseball and raced jumping bullfrogs. Grayson couldn't be bothered with the actions of children around him. By the time he turned sixteen, Grayson's summers were taken up working odd jobs, checking off the daily monotony of a list of chores left by Father on the note board in the kitchen, and Faith. Grayson and Faith met in the sixth grade and became friends. Aside from a few other school acquaintances, Grayson functioned well enough on his own. By the time he and Faith were eighteen, their time together grew into a comfortable relationship.

When Grayson announced their engagement, while attending a local business college, neither family was surprised. On the night before the wedding, Grayson's father approached him. "Grayson, your future is at hand. I know you are a hard worker and would never want anything simply given to you. We are a lot alike in that way, Son. Your mother and I had always planned that at least one of our children would continue in the family business. I will give you the opportunity to buy into the corporation. Think about it, and if you do consider my offer, just let me know how many shares you'd like to purchase."

Then and there, Grayson decided that he and his wife would set out on their own. He needed no one's charity, especially from that overlord. The small offering was nothing compared to what Grayson would earn and the man he would become. Let his brother beg from the pompous, old man—but not Grayson.

He went back home, twice: the first time was for Annabeth's wedding and the second for his brother's funeral after a tragic car accident. There was quiet talk of alcohol being a factor in the crash. When his own father died, Grayson sent flowers.

Although there was an inheritance, Annabeth and her husband controlled most of the shares. Grayson had little communication with his sister after that, other than an occasional phone call when a new niece or nephew was born. Christmas cards were exchanged each winter; formalities and particulars were in step with Grayson's style.

Grayson's professional life was full, but wealth was not enough. The power and control, which came from making judicious decisions, were addictive. He could no more take a vacation from work than he could stop Faith from asking for a divorce. Their two girls, Elizabeth and Claire, would be well-cared for. Faith was too meek to demand much more. Years later, he heard that she was happily married to a man who chartered fishing trips in Florida—probably to tourists in flowered shirts searching for their life's dream of having a wall mount of "the big one"—a total waste, thought Grayson, shaking his head. He just couldn't understand trivialities.

QUESTIONS AND REFLECTIONS:

Think about a childhood experience that molded you. As you grew older, did that experience continue to change you, or was the effect just in that moment?

Can you relate to Grayson's professional work ethic, either personally or through someone else? How does that contribute to you as a person, family member, church member, community member, employee, or employer?

CHAPTER Three

"Mister—Hey Mister!" Grayson turned quickly, not quite startled, yet the broken silence was as much a relief from the past as an intrusion. A young girl, hair in braids and dressed in shorts, shirt, and sandals, held out a small ball, "Want to play?"

"Uh, no, thank you. Where are your parents?"

"My Father is everywhere," she replied, brightly. "C'mon, let's play catch. I'll teach you."

"I know how to play; I just do not play."

"But why not?" she mused.

"I just don't," added Grayson in a stern tone.

"Why not?" she insisted.

Grayson, trying to be patient, retorted, "Your parents will be worried about you."

"Do you worry about your children?" the little girl pried and then disappeared around a corner.

Grayson considered following her, just to make sure she was safely back in the hands of a parent or guardian. What business was it of his anyway? It was of no concern to him. After all, he had to get back to what he was doing. This was carefully planned time. He was still a very busy man. As Grayson backtracked toward the corridor he had been traveling, he heard the sound of a muffled giggle from a distant room. A rubber ball slowly rolled toward and then past him. "Silly child," he quietly sighed aloud. The star and polka dot markings on the ball looked oddly familiar.

As he walked on, Grayson came to a balcony of sorts. He saw no staircase below, however, he watched intently from above as a few women arranged chairs and white bows. A small altar had been set in front of the seats. The flowers and matching satin bows and ribbons gave an impression that the room would be used to hold a wedding. It must be a way for the museum to add to its annual revenue, thought Grayson. Maybe they hold weddings after hours or on off days. Grayson would be the last person to argue about increasing income for any business. After all, there were not many other visitors in the museum, that day. As the women scurried back and forth, Grayson was drawn to their sense of purpose. He wondered whether they were friends or relatives of the couple or perhaps worked for the museum itself. They did not wear uniforms but appeared rather similar morphologically as well as in age and even hair color. Grayson turned away, no longer interested.

The next hallway housed textiles. Most were hanging on simple frames or propped up against self-standing easels. One, in particular, caught his eye—a multi-colored tapestry. It was titled, "Suffering in Africa." Grayson found himself studying patterns in the yarn, interconnected as the colors were woven throughout. The more intently Grayson stared, the greater the pull. He began to imagine the sound of drums. He could almost hear voices; perhaps it was chanting. There were men and women, each busy at a specific task. And then, he saw her while squinting slightly as if to get a closer look at the details. She was a beautiful, dark-skinned woman with her head wrapped in cloth and hair totally hidden. She wore make-up or perhaps her face was painted. The layers of her dress draped her shoulders, hips, and legs. She was seated in front of a hut. As Grayson focused, he could see the thatch and even strips of bark and tree saplings, all assimilated into one piece. It was a home, a place that could offer shade from the sweltering heat and shelter during the soaking rains. It could not, however, afford protection from what he would witness next.

In the woman's arms, lay a lifeless form, swaddled by a thin, rough-looking cloth and flies—at first, he believed the insects to be the actual features of the child. Grayson assumed the woman was the mother. She was crying softly. There were other children around her, and a thin boy of twelve or so had his hand placed decisively on the woman's shoulder. Smaller children sat at her feet; a toddler balanced on her lap; and a young girl leaned her head against the woman's side. Yes, the group must certainly be family, he surmised. An odor, no, a stench began to rise from the scene. Grayson knew the smell, although he had never before experienced it in his lifetime. The acrid odors of death and disease reeked from the upright rug. Each colorful pattern had purpose as together, they lifted the songs, prayers, and tears from that distant land of a people so long ago.

Grayson desired to turn and walk away. He was uncomfortable. No more double martinis at lunch, he thought as he adjusted his suit jacket and tie, in an attempt to shake off the experience. Maybe he should follow up with his doctor, who had been trying to get him to submit to a full physical and lab work for some time. He'd have his secretary schedule an appointment the following week. Pulling away and walking into another hallway, Grayson was sure he heard a subdued cry. "So strange," he said aloud.

QUESTIONS AND REFLECTIONS:

Why is play so important and so easy for children? In Grayson's line, "I know how to play; I just do not play," what does that say to you? Do you know others with this mindset? How do or would you react to the child and to Grayson? Think about and discuss the relevance of the reactions of both characters.

Allow yourself to enter into the tapestry titled, "Suffering in Africa." Spend time with the woman, her family, the deceased baby, and the surroundings, permitting contact with and the permeation of your senses. What do you notice?

CHAPTER *Four*

Grayson realized that he was perspiring and slightly short of breath. It was not the same as from a friendly game of racquetball or even the morning jog he often made time for. Many associates commented about the high level of fitness he maintained at his age. "Calm down, Gray Man," he said out loud and deliberately adjusted his respirations. Grayson often coached himself that way during challenges. He remembered, one time in the past, first nervously thinking about but then reassuring himself that his creative investment plan might lead to an inside trading indictment. He knew enough lawyers, investment experts, and judges to ward that off. "One could never be too careful, eh, Son?" he chuckled to himself.

Sam Parry, one of Grayson's top executives, nervously waited to be called in by the secretary. "Mr. Grayson will see you, now, Mr. Parry." Sam was a shrewd businessman and hand-picked by Grayson because of it. As Sam entered the office, he looked around at the familiar décor. Everything was in its place, as usual. Grayson sat behind the cherry-colored stained and highly polished mahogany desk, motioning Sam with a well-manicured hand to take a seat across from him. With the exception of a few carefully placed keepsakes, Parry often wondered how a man of such importance would have so little apparent work; no papers, files, or planner were ever noticeable. Must have others doing it all behind-the-scenes, he thought. Grayson always appeared mannequin-like to Parry. His hair, suit, tie, cufflinks, shoes, and socks were immaculately chosen. His expression was always controlled.

"Parry," began Grayson, "you know how I've always depended on you." There was an uncomfortable silence, a pause, which felt like eternity to Sam Parry.

"Yes, sir."

"I will not mince words," Grayson crooned. "The time has come for you to retire. Your job here is done. You have been well compensated for your part in the last two transactions. Your severance will be healthy. You'll be set for the future."

"Thank you, sir, for the opportunity to have been of service to you and your company," hesitated Parry.

"You have been helpful, Parry, very helpful. Our agreement has been completed."

As Parry stood to leave, he started, "Just in case, sir—"

"—It has been concluded, thank you, Mr. Parry. Oh, and Sam, in the event you choose to talk, you'll never work again. You won't know what hit you. Your family would seriously miss you. I am certain you wouldn't want them to suffer."

"Uh, thank you, sir."

As the door opened and closed again, Grayson sat, hands folded, nodding.

Chapter Four

QUESTIONS AND REFLECTIONS:

How or when have you seen yourself in Grayson? What were the positives and negatives? Did being like Grayson result in change? If given the opportunity to be in that same position again, might you alter anything?

How or when have you been like Sam Parry? What were the positives and negatives? Did being like Sam Parry result in change? If given the opportunity to be in that same position again, might you alter anything?

CHAPTER
Five

Grayson walked around the corner. He needed to wrap up this day of cultural sight-seeing. He continued for a time, passing corridors recognized, as well as unrecognized. "For Pete's sake," he muttered, "where did I come in?" A clearing at the end of the hall revealed a slight illumination. Grayson approached, hoping for a familiar passageway or at the very least, an exit sign. As he looked out and through an open alcove, there it was again, the very same room with wedding preparations, situated on the floor below. The women were still busy with whatever they had been doing, although the scene looked precisely the same as it had an hour or so before. Grayson wondered, how long had it been exactly?

He leaned over and cleared his throat, "Ah, excuse me …" No response came back. "Excuse me, madams, which way would be the exit? I'm rather in a hurry," Grayson's voice resonated, but it was as if he was invisible and silent. "Insolent women! I should file a complaint!"

Grayson turned and moved through another hallway. Viewing a sign above, he unexpectedly stopped in his tracks and whispered, "North American Early Cultures." He had almost forgotten that this was a museum, not just an art exhibit. Bowls, arrowheads, tools, jewelry, and other artifacts surrounded by skins and furs beckoned him. Affixed to the partitions,

Chapter Five

he spotted a group of restored sepia-tone photographs depicting Native American tribal members that were dated circa 1880 – 1910. One, in particular, caught his attention. It was a photograph of a young woman with what resembled powdered paint spread all over her face. The caption simply read, "Apache Sunrise Dance, Arizona."

"Most impressive," exhaled Grayson, as he wondered about the people in the photographs and their stories. He methodically walked through a re-created village that took up an entire adjoining room. A horizontal, raised structure stood purposefully apart from the scale-model community. His desire to turn and walk away was strong, but he lingered, unmoving. Drums, quiet and distant at first, sounded slightly closer as Grayson looked up toward the burial scaffold. A form, tightly wrapped in skins, rested atop. There must be a motion sensor that starts the drum sounds, he thought, or perhaps, it was timed at intervals. "Clever …" Grayson said aloud but quickly stopped when he detected the odor of smoke. It was not actually the scent of wood burning but more like the heavy fragrance of incense he remembered from church services as a young boy, when Mama would hold his hand as he squirmed in the pew. It was difficult to recall details, but his senses evoked memories.

The male voice was quiet, gentle. "Grayson, these people treated each other well. They were family in the deepest sense of the word. Even the dead were highly respected. Learn from this now, before it is too late. These people suffered great injustices, yet continued in their ways as long as they could. For some, death was a freedom that life could not promise."

"Father?" Grayson asked out loud.

"Grayson, learn from this now, before it is too late."

"Where are you, Father—Dad?"

"I am here; I am with you. My mistakes became your mistakes. Learn and grow now, and your time here will be useful."

The drums were once again barely audible. Had they continued to sound the whole time? Why this room? Why his own father's voice? "This has been a most bizarre day, most bizarre … quite the understatement," Grayson whispered.

QUESTIONS AND REFLECTIONS:

If you had the opportunity, what would you ask or say to Grayson?

If you were in Grayson's place, where would you go next? What questions might you be asking? Would you attempt to make sense of what Grayson deemed, "a bizarre day?" How do the senses evoke memories and sentiments?

CHAPTER Six

As Grayson walked past the same, familiar room, he finally saw a sign for the exit, next to "Grand Ballroom." He followed the only path and descended a staircase. Entering the space, he immediately recognized the area that had been set for what he could only figure was a wedding. The women were no longer present. As he walked along the center aisle, set between the rows of chairs on the left and the right, Grayson approached the altar where the bride and groom would ceremoniously stand. The place looked the same from this angle except for the large cross at the foremost end of the hall where the bride and groom would present themselves to God.

The word sounded strange. It had been so long since he had used it, well, not as an expletive or as his mother would have remarked, "in vain." He reviewed the mental slide show of times he sat in a church pew with Mama and his siblings, never really noticing the word one way or another.

Grayson whispered it, "God," and again, but this time a bit louder, "God." Funny, how that word slipped in and out of his oral vocabulary. Maybe people say it when they really need something, he thought, like, God, please help me, or oh, God, I need a cigarette, or my God, a shot of whiskey would be great right about now.

What was that scent? Grayson was met with a sense of recognition. It was slightly woody with a hint of citrus. He hadn't experienced it in a very long time, but it was unmistakable. Even after all these years, Grayson would always know the smell of his father's aftershave lotion.

Grayson, still lost in thought, looked up at the cross and then back around the room and imagined the wedding scene. Two people would stand before representational clergy of some denomination and make a promise to their Maker. "Promises likely to be broken should never be made," Grayson said aloud. A simple statement with complex ramifications, it was always complicated, thought Grayson. His first marriage was such. His second had been one of convenience—

"—and your third, Son, never really was. What was she, twenty … twenty-five years younger than you?"

"Just be quiet, Dad! Wait a minute, is that really you, Father? Why can't I see you? It's because you're not really here!" Emotion welled within Grayson. "You have no jurisdiction over me, no control."

"No, Son, just pity and a small portion of hope."

Grayson looked around twice, not quite sure what he would or would not see. He prided himself on not showing anger. He was in fact, highly annoyed yet a bit surprised that he had just shouted out loud at something nonexistent. His father had been dead for years. How could this be? He was beginning to accept that little of the day would ever be understood. Grayson mentally affirmed the plan to call his doctor and make an overdue appointment. It was probably just stress. After all, he had always been strong-minded. That trait ran on his father's side of the family. His mother was easy-going, as was his sister and what he remembered of their brother. Dad was not so much strong-willed as stubborn. Once he made up his mind, which was about the same time the idea popped into his head, there was no changing it.

When his father assumed that a hunting experience would create some kind of connection between the two, Grayson found himself at an outfitter with all the equipment any young man could dream about owning. After almost shooting himself in the foot, Grayson found that he was the target of his father's wrath. He had always wondered whether Father was disappointed in him or simply never wanted to experience having to explain some tragic event to Mama.

They both agreed to retire to the tent for the evening. The nightlong rain created a deluge. The tent was thoroughly soaked through, as were their clothes and equipment. Grayson woke with a terrible cough, fever, and chills. After recovering from near pneumonia, it was agreed that the boy's hunting days would end as abruptly as they had begun. Grayson's father never mentioned the experience or even the sport, again. For a while, the son had wished they could have at least talked about it. Not that he ever really wanted to actually shoot any warm-blooded creature, Grayson preferred his steaks to be restaurant cuts, specially prepared to his liking. Still, understanding exactly where he stood with his father would have been better than never really knowing. It wasn't ever black or white, just grey. Did Father hate him, or was he simply dissatisfied with the eldest? Was there some shadow of blood-related love? After all, Father must have loved Mama, but so little emotion was ever displayed. Grayson maintained that his father must have at least cared. Grayson continued from the Grand Ballroom to the exit.

QUESTIONS AND REFLECTIONS:

Say the word, "God," out loud as Grayson has done. How do you feel? What thoughts or images form? Do you speak with God, ask him questions, or beg him when in troubling times? How does God respond?

Why does seeing a cross make Grayson think about broken promises? What images, symbols, or icons are powerful in your life?

PART II
DESCENT

CHAPTER
Seven

Grayson opened the heavy metal door by pushing a horizontal release bar. The sign above the access was clearly marked, "Exit." He walked out, and the door shut behind him. There must be some sort of mistake, he thought. Before him was a tube, a tunnel of sorts. At first, Grayson thought he was finally outside but then wondered if this was still part of the museum. The walls were covered with old, yellow tile, greyed with age and upheld by soot-stained grout. It resembled the subways he rode for years underneath the city. The details were impeccable. It smelled of cigarettes, old food, and yes, he thought, even a faint scent of urine. Grayson was not in the least bit curious about how that was infused. "Could this really be a mural?" he mused. Although Grayson was not quite sure of his whereabouts, he appreciated the clever design.

His eyes followed the upward and curved lines of the wall, and he observed in amazement that the tunnel had painted lighting, actually shielded by wire mesh. The light bulbs within their protective cages were even glazed with dust and grime. The reality of the art was stunning. It reminded him of a movie soundstage he once visited where even the old gum on the sidewalks looked real. As Grayson cast his eyes downward, he was astonished by the perspective with which the train tracks were displayed. The stairs that a passenger would use to climb aboard the train appeared three-dimensional. He had to convince himself; Grayson bent down and ran a hand over one of the steps. It was flat, two-dimensionally flat! Fantastic! Before he was able to stand up straight, Grayson heard the roar of a train and felt a strong, warm breeze that carried an oily trace in its wake.

He turned back to the metal door through which he departed the museum proper. He tried to open it. There was no handle on his side. The door could not be pried; it was locked. Not one to panic, Grayson turned to face the tracks once again. Interesting, he thought. He stepped forward. The roar had become a clanging and could still be heard in the absence of anything seen.

As Grayson walked over the two-dimensional step, he was suddenly thrown forward and then to the side. He tried to reorient himself and regain his balance. Everything around him became pitch black except for the flashing lights his eyes and brain recorded. He sensed the strong swaying motion as if he was inside a train car, moving quickly along a track—but to where? The alternating blinking lights replicated precisely that which could be viewed from a subway window as the train passed by brightly lit bulbs in the darkness of the passage. How that took him back to his late-night commutes home! He looked around but did not see the interior of a train. Yet, he truly felt the motion and continued to see flashing lights.

The sensation of the moving car slowed to a stop. Grayson was as equally relieved as he was hesitant of what would come next. He heard an all too familiar noise from his commuter past, the sound of two metal subway doors squeaking and sliding open. He had ridden countless times on subway trains and often marveled at how those metal doors, fitted with oblong glass windows mounted within curved corners, functioned time after time. He automatically stepped forward from the non-train. The sound of the portals closing behind him, the grind of the wheels on the track, the growl of the monster pulling its own weight, and once again, the wind from its wake had passed him.

Grayson looked up and just above eye-level, etched into the aged, yellowed wall tile, he saw the words in capital letters, "FOR WE OURSELVES." Interesting, decided Grayson.

QUESTIONS AND REFLECTIONS:

Do you feel relief or frustration at Grayson being able to exit the museum? If you place yourself in Grayson's shoes, how might you react? What would you do? How does this scenario simulate life's events?

How does "FOR WE OURSELVES" speak to you?

CHAPTER
Eight

Grayson turned and walked parallel to the rails. Funny how art can play tricks on the mind, he considered. The tunnel and tracks continued. Grayson was sure that if he followed them, the lines painted to resemble train tracks would certainly narrow, reflecting frame of reference. They actually appeared to curve slightly in the dimly lit distance. He remained on the path. Two young boys, eight or nine years of age, became visible at the bend. They neared Grayson and pointed at him, looked at each other, laughed and continued past him. As Grayson turned around to look behind, he thought that perhaps he could inquire in regards to their whereabouts and give each boy a quarter for their help. They were gone. How could that be? The stretch from where he just originated went on as far as the eye could see.

He journeyed for an indeterminate amount of time. "I've seen both those young men before—but where? Now I'm talking out loud to myself; this is not a good sign."

Grayson heard something faint. It sounded like a single strain. Yes, it was the sound of a musical instrument. On the sidewalk ahead in the distance, Grayson suddenly noticed a bundle where the melody must certainly have been originating. As he approached, the image became a man in a long, dark, and tattered coat. He wore a stretched scarf around his neck, so dirty that one could not tell its original color. The man's head was covered with a knitted cap, nestled just above the top of his eyes, concealing the eyebrows. Grayson could not tell the color, length or even the existence of the man's hair. It was obscured by cap, scarf, and coat, which all merged together into one piece. The man wore a full beard, which was mostly grey, except for traces of curly black wisps. He sat on a vertically set, rectangular wooden crate, his back against the dingy, yellow tiled wall, holding a stringed instrument. The cello's thin stand was planted on the discolored walkway. Its operator, a visible contrast to the instrument, caressed the neck of the cello with his left hand. The bow was held precisely in the right. An eerie, melodic sound flowed from the four strings. Grayson admired the beautifully finished wood, the delicate scrollwork, wooden tuning pegs, specifically set strings, and elegantly cut italic letter F-shaped holes, where sound resonated and emerged. Grayson searched for the inevitable cup on the floor. It was metal and reminded him of tin cups used by prisoners in old black and white movies as they'd be raked across bars of the jail cells to call the attention of the guards.

The man continued to play the haunting piece. Grayson was quickly enchanted by the music. It conjured up a myriad of images from his past. During the summer when he was eight, Grayson's father convinced Mama that their son needed to grow up a bit. "You'll see," he told his wife, "it'll make a man out of him." As Father dropped Grayson off at the camp, he asserted, "See you in two weeks, Son," and held out his hand for the youth to shake. As the car door closed, Grayson, holding onto the handle of a small valise, could still hear the classical music his father had playing on the AM radio in the vehicle. Grayson swore that the music continued to be perceptible as he watched the car shrink smaller and smaller into the distance.

Grayson did not have much in common with the other campers. He was picked last for teams, couldn't paddle his canoe in a synchronized fashion, and was unwanted in tug-of-war, except when they needed a smaller fellow up front near the ribbon, to be pulled headlong into the mud. The other children had either laughed at Grayson or politely ignored him. On that first night, Grayson buried his head in the pillow, unable to stop thinking about how much he loved Mama and how much he despised his father. As he cried himself to sleep, Grayson was determined that he would never let anyone see his weaknesses again. He would make himself strong in every way. Not only would he show them, he'd own them, and if need be, he would make them suffer. The man in the making swore a solemn vow that night. Others would beg to have portions of his attention, his money, and his power.

That's it, he thought! Those two boys were there with him at summer camp, so many years ago. For what reason had he just envisioned such an image from his past? The music disconcertingly played on. Grayson found it to be intoxicating. He bent down to put a coin into the tin cup in hopes of continuing on. When he reached first into the pocket of his pants and then his coat, Grayson found nothing, no coins, no bills, not even his money clip. Grayson concluded that he had either been robbed or should be committed. The man looked up, and Grayson's eyes met a set of large, dark, hollow orbs. Grayson jumped back and gasped.

The man slowly encountered Grayson's gaze. A deep and gravelly voice commanded, "Forgive, Gravescend; the key I give you is to forgive."

"My name is Grayson," he indignantly responded.

"Forgive everyone, Gravescend."

"Absurd," he scoffed and was suddenly back on the train.

QUESTIONS AND REFLECTIONS:

If you permit yourself to walk along with Grayson, what thoughts or feelings do you experience? If you do not enter into the tunnel with Grayson, what prevents you from doing so? Where might you go instead? Grayson is analytical yet does not always question the remarkable. What reasoning might explain this?

What are your impressions of the cellist? Does his presenting Grayson with the "key to forgive" seem relevant? How might the renaming of Grayson to Gravescend be meaningful? What would you share with the main character about this? Has anyone ever mistaken your name? How did it affect you or the situation?

CHAPTER Nine

The swaying motion, combined with the sensation of moving at high speed was remarkable. He could not put an end to the images of the cello player. The music, his dress, the eyes, his command to forgive, and Grayson's renaming—perhaps it meant something, he contemplated. Grayson absentmindedly put a hand into his pocket once again and was instantly reminded that it was empty. His watch and other belongings were still missing. What appeared to be real might be unreal. Where was his money or for that matter, the museum ticket handed to him by the uniformed gentleman at the entrance? Even as a child and then a young man, Grayson always carried spare cash and kept impeccable track of his possessions.

He and Faith would often laugh in their younger days. She would tease him about being too frugal. He'd matter-of-factly remind her that their level of comfort was due to hard work in conjunction with being prudent. Faith knew that her husband never shied away from hard work. She would sometimes say that the only time her husband would not have money in his pocket would be when he'd meet St. Peter at the Pearly Gates.

The strobe effect of the lights slowed and finally stopped. The train, although Grayson still could not see anything that looked like a subway car, screeched to a halt. He again heard the sound of the metal doors and instinctively stepped forward and looked up for a sign. "In Debt to Us" was etched and stood out from the tile as if it was an ancient relief carved in stone.

He turned quickly as the pleasant sound of Faith's voice danced across the stale air of the subway tunnel. "Faith," he gasped. The singing continued. "Faith," he repeated, pleadingly. Oh, how he loved and missed that woman, except in life, he had rarely expressed his affection. "In life," he whispered. "She's been gone so long." He found himself choked up.

"Gravescend, go up, not down." It was his beloved's sweet, sweet voice, once again after so many years. Her voice was like rich, sweet nectar, beckoning and cajoling him from the depth of his soul.

"Faith—where are you?"

"Gravescend, you can still change …" her voice trailed.

"Why are you calling me that?" he demanded.

"Change … I am not of this place, Gravescend … change, and join me." She was gone.

He felt total abandonment in being asked to do the impossible. After all, she was no longer present but in his past. Hearing his father's voice earlier was one thing. However, sensing Faith's voice, sounding sweet and clear as a bell … all he wanted to do was reach out and hold her, but he could not. Where was she? Where was he? The pain of her loss then, which he never permitted himself to feel, was now upon his soul. Although they had been divorced for years when she passed, the wasted and untouched emotions besieged him. It was unbearable, and Gravescend began to weep and then sob as he slowly emptied himself within the surreal tunnel.

QUESTIONS AND REFLECTIONS:

What are the possible meanings of the etched message, "In Debt to Us?" Why is the main character now called Gravescend?

How do we recognize a call to change? Faith pleads, "Change … I am not of this place, Gravescend … change, and join me." Why does Gravescend feel that he is being asked to do the impossible? Where is Faith? Where is Gravescend? Who or what has the capacity to call us to change and then, willfully make that transformation?

CHAPTER Ten

When he awoke, Gravescend was spent. He reasoned that he must have cried for a long time, even though he had not shed tears since childhood. The memories flooded back and were temporarily suspended by the aroma of freshly baked bread. It was wonderful! He was still in the train station or whatever the place or time or realm was. His grandmother, who he had lived with during his twelfth summer, was standing there, silver hair bun, blue plaid dress, and white apron, all perfectly in place. That is exactly how he remembered her, except she looked somehow younger, less worn.

"Graveson ..." she started.

"... Gravescend; I mean, Grayson," he interjected, shaking his head back and forth.

"Son, please do not interrupt. I do not have much time with you. We have been given this opportunity because it is not too late. You need to pay attention, Grandson. Forgive those who have left you, have hurt you, and have disappointed you, and you will not be disappointed, ever again. Go back to the Gallery and walk the walk as you should have."

"I would if it meant getting out of here, but how is that possible, Grandmother? Grandmother!"

Chapter Ten

She was gone, and he was back on the train. It was once again moving swiftly and stopped in front of what appeared to be an elevator, waiting with open doors. The grave man stepped away from the train and into the elevator. The doors sealed smoothly and silently.

Graveson was immediately greeted by a much older gentleman in a uniform, who asked which floor he wanted. The interior of the elevator was exquisite. The walls and floors must be Italian marble, he theorized, while the hardware and accents were brass. As he looked up, an old-fashioned semicircular dial, pointing toward the numbers, marked the floor they were on.

"Sir?"

"Gallery, please," the doors opened, and he stepped out. "Of course," sighed Graveson. The women were busy below, scurrying around the white chairs and decorations. They must be preparing for a wedding, thought Graveson with a sigh of resignation.

How long have I been here, he wondered? I know I am at the city museum, but where am I, exactly? How long must I stay here? I might actually need a measure of assistance—something he was not accustomed to. "Yes, help," he said aloud. The word imprisonment came to his mind. Ridiculous! Or, was it? Upon thinking that, he came upon a sizable mosaic made of small colored glass tiles. A man behind bars was the artist's subject. Outside the bars, another man or actually, only the arm of a man holding a key in his outstretched hand could be seen from the artist's angle. The prisoner, on his knees, was reaching with both hands extended and with a look of longing and pain on his face. Hmm, thought Graveson, again, the key.

What was the key, according to the man with the cello? Who or what must I forgive? Is that my key to getting out of here? The concept that Graveson was unable to leave was becoming tangible. Reminders of the most recent day or days or hours, minutes, or seconds suddenly flooded his mind:

"Learn from this now, before it is too late."

"Forgive everyone."

"Change."

"Go up, not down."

"In Debt to Us,"

"For We Ourselves,"

Exasperated, he wondered and spoke quietly; it was almost imperceptible, "And why can't anyone get my name right?"

Looking again at the tiles creating the picture, Graveson noticed finer details. Opposite the man on the interior wall of the jail cell, there was a window inside the prison chamber. That too, had bars. Beyond the barricaded opening, there was a bird. It was in the distance from the viewer's perspective, but one could unmistakably tell that it was indeed a rather large bird at that. The animal's relative size could be compared to the bough of a large tree upon which it sat. Graveson was drawn to that minute feature.

The bird was full-bodied with a short-rounded head, dark eyes, and brown striations on its side, which beautifully stood out from the white underbelly. The brown wings were closed, yet strong and sturdy. This was some kind of eagle; no, it was a hawk, he reconsidered. The one eye on the visible side of the painting seemed to focus both on the prisoner, or rather, the criminal and Graveson.

And then, Graveson was suddenly looking upon the bird, an actual living creature, not even an arm's length from him, perched on the wooden frame of the mosaic. A beautiful female voice emerged from the hawk. She sang in a human voice and introduced herself as Lily. "I can lead you," she sang. "Follow me to a place where you dare not permit yourself to journey. Do you wish to ascend or descend?"

"What difference does it mat—why, ascend, of course," he added, remembering Faith's beautiful voice, scarcely believing he was conversing with a bird.

"Go up, it shall be. The choice is and has always been yours, Gray-Sin." He saw a new name etched below the mosaic in the title of the work, "Man Imprisoned in Gray Sin."

"What is this gray sin?" he slowly questioned with eyes downcast and looking away from the art piece and away from Lily.

"Sin never accounted for," she sang.

"Well then, it is not sin," retorted the man.

Chapter Ten

"Then, why have you imprisoned yourself?" asked the bird. As the man looked up, he suddenly recognized the incarcerated figure in the picture as himself. Gray-Sin quickly and forcefully recoiled away from picture, the bird, and himself.

QUESTIONS AND REFLECTIONS:

Think about or discuss the significance of the primary character meeting those who have passed on. He hears his father's voice, that of his ex-wife, and actually sees his grandmother. What do they want him to do? What might be his interpretation? What are the implications of more names for this man?

How do we imprison ourselves in "gray sin" or "sin never accounted for," as explained by Lily, a hawk? Why might Gray-Sin meet a talking bird? Should he trust her? Would you? What might Lily represent to this detained person? Does one need to recognize confinement in order to be imprisoned?

CHAPTER
Eleven

*S*tumbling backward, Gray-Sin tripped and fell, hitting his head against the wall and biting into his lower lip. He reached first, for his mouth and then skull. No blood, that's good he thought, although it surprised him. How could any of this be, he silently questioned?

As he stood up, Gray-Sin felt drawn to enter another room. It was decorated with nostalgia from the 1940s and 50s. Complete with living room furniture, he spotted a sofa with the patterning so familiar, he could have sworn and almost wished it were from his parents' own home during his childhood. The black and white television, sporting a set of rabbit ears antenna, was on and playing.

Gray-Sin couldn't resist the temptation and sank into the sofa, making himself quite comfortable. He noticed the stack of snack tray tables neatly hung on the matching storage stand alongside the couch and felt strangely cozy. The picture on the old T.V. tube was at first, a set of horizontal and then vertical lines. Suddenly, the image became clearer. Gray-Sin was staring at a much younger version of himself, walking home from the subway station on a cold, dark, autumn night. He heard whimpering and quiet moaning. The memory flooded back into his mind as if it had just occurred. She was young, her clothes torn, and she was lying, crumpled in her own blood. The woman had apparently gone through something awful. As she sputtered out to him, Grayson crossed the street and kept walking, eyes focused ahead, never turning back.

"Oh …" he groaned, realizing his mistake from so many years prior.

"Sin never accounted for," he heard Lily's voice in his head.

The television set was playing, again. This time, he was a boy of ten in Miss Woodrie's classroom. That he could even remember her name was striking to him. Miss Woodrie was kind and gentle. Her crystalline blue-grey eyes would laugh as the children responded in class. She even had the group put on a play and insisted that every student take a role in the production. Miss Woodrie was his favorite teacher in elementary school. She knew that he was a very bright and talented boy. At the age of ten, he thought she was the most beautiful woman, apart from his own mother, that he had ever seen. She wore little jewelry, but his eyes were often drawn to a small gold pendant of the perfectly balanced Scales of Justice, fastened by a thin chain around her delicate neck.

The day she caught him cheating on an exam was the lowest day in his school life and in the first decade of his existence. Gray-Sin viewed himself on the T.V. screen as Miss Woodrie walked by his desk and whispered, "Grayson, I'd like to have a word with you at recess." His heart must have stopped momentarily. Sweat broke out on his upper lip and then his forehead. Keep cool, Gray, he had thought to himself.

Standing in front of Miss Woodrie's desk after the other pupils had exited for lunch, he felt a deep sense of embarrassment as well as an unexpected emotion—defiance. "No, ma'am," he lied to her. "There must be some mistake. I bet you saw Tommy and thought it was me. I did not cheat. I always get good grades!"

Miss Woodrie might have second-guessed herself but barely for a moment. She tilted her head slowly and announced, "Young man, cheating is lying, and lying is a serious offense. You hurt only yourself by such actions. Now, since this is the first time, I will not inform your mother or father. However, if such an event occurs again, we will all meet together to decide what actions should be taken."

"Yes, ma'am," was all that emanated from his mouth, while simultaneously thinking, you'll need to be more careful next time, Gray. As Gray-Sin watched the television in what was now to be described as definite discomfort, he was able to hear his own words and thoughts on screen.

Miss Woodrie broke through, "You are excused and may join the others at recess," she directed.

He watched himself pick up his lunch pail and a small speckled ball encircled with stars and walk out through the classroom door. Just being a kid, he ineffectively tried to convince himself. Gray-Sin considered changing the channel but instead, stood up and walked away.

QUESTIONS AND REFLECTIONS:

What is the significance of Gray-Sin's surprise at the lack of blood after his hard fall?

How might the scene with Miss Woodrie have affected the boy's life? Did it have an ultimate impact? Was it either positive or negative?

CHAPTER
Twelve

Gray-Sin stepped briskly. His goal was no longer locating an exit. It was simply to leave. He considered trying to open a window and use the fire escape. He needed to get away from the voices, the images, and the gnawing feeling that he had done something terribly wrong. It had been a very long time since that was a part of his life. Guilt was something perceived by the weaker of the species, he concluded.

He was absorbed in thought until interrupted by a mural of sorts. It was a self-standing tri-pieced work of art. All three panels were the same height, which was about five feet tall by Gray-Sin's estimate. The center section was close to three feet wide, while the left and right pieces, all hinged together by three separate wooden frames, were each half the width, perhaps about eighteen inches across, he assessed, trying to grasp onto reality. Numbers and math always made sense, he theorized.

On the left panel, there was a striking resemblance to the beautiful African woman with the dying baby that he experienced in the tapestry earlier in the day. In the center panel, he recognized the same woman, reaching out in desperation, partially on her knees and being held back by two men, all dressed in similarly draped garments. It was dark, probably nighttime. Her tears were highlighted by the glow of the moon as they ran down her face. The two younger children were each clinging to their mother. Expressions of terror permeated their tear-filled eyes. The authenticity of the lighting was stunning.

There was still another cause for her pain, and it was depicted on the third board. The older boy, most likely in his early teens, was shackled and being dragged off by thieves. Unmistakable slave-traders carried nets, whips, and other weapons. Gray-Sin could hear the helpless maternal screams and feel the boy's agony. Long lines of dark-skinned men, young and old, were bound by chains, prodded and led. The scene was reflected by the indirect lighting as they slowly made their way to small boats on the shore. The mother ship rested in the distant waters, awaiting its predestined cargo.

"Do you wish to enter the scene and change their fate?" asked the voice.

"Wha—what? Excuse me?" mumbled Gray-Sin.

"Do you wish to enter the scene and change their future?" clarified the questioning voice. It was that nagging hawk again, although Gray-Sin could not see her.

Gray-Sin spun and walked away. The familiar polka-dotted, starry ball rolled past his feet. The young girl from earlier in the day stepped out in front of him as he approached another hallway. "The angel-hawk has asked you a question. Won't you play?"

"Who are you?" he asked with curiosity, obviously unamused.

"I am Averee Child," she answered with confidence yet in disbelief that Gray-Sin was unfamiliar with her. "Of course, you know me," the girl continued.

He shook his head and looked away, "We've never met."

"Ohhhh, but we haaaavvve," she playfully exaggerated. "We were once very close, long ago …" her voice trailed off and then pleaded in a womanly tone, "… I am both the embodiment and the culmination of youth." Without question or comment, he twisted direction and passed into another room, never looking back at the once playful child.

The wedding scene, thought Gray-Sin without conceding any emotion. It was all the same, once again. The white chairs remained perfectly aligned, the snowy bows and ribbons rested upon the end of each row, and the cross

Chapter Twelve

stood, large and looming. Gray-Sin walked up to the front of the room once again and was almost knocked off balance by what he witnessed.

Kneeling at the foot of the cross was—no, it couldn't be—it was Parry. "Sam!" Gray-Sin raised his voice, almost shouting, surprised and thrilled to see someone he knew. Parry knelt, looking skyward, his lips silently moving. Gray-Sin stepped closer. "Parry, come on! Sam, it's me."

Sam began to whisper, "Yes, Lord, I do forgive." Parry stared upward and beyond the cross. As Gray-Sin permitted his eyes to follow Sam's, he realized that it was no ordinary cross. It had become a life-sized crucifix with a life-sized image of Jesus Christ impaled through the wood. Gray-Sin's focus dropped to Sam Parry's face. As Gray-Sin's glance fell upon the features of his old employee, a drop of blood from above spattered onto Parry's forehead and dripped slowly around one eye and then over his cheekbone onto the side of the face in the track where his own tear could trace a similar route, determined by angle and gravity. Gray-Sin speculated, why this likeness? Parry never removed his gaze from the God-figure. Something in Gray-Sin wanted to reach out and just let Sam know he could be there for him. Nevertheless, he decided to leave Parry alone.

Some years after Parry had left the firm, Gray-Sin heard that Sam had made some poor investments and first, lost his home and then, his family. In the cool of spring that still mimics winter in the air and smells of newness, Gray-Sin's secretary called on the intercom to let him know that Sam Parry stopped by to request a visit. She softly intoned that he looked quite rough and disheveled. Gray-Sin instructed her to tell Parry that he was unavailable to see him, and it would be best if he would leave on his own, that was, without an escort.

A few months later, Gray-Sin had read the obituary in the newspaper. What a fool, he reflected. Sam might have been comfortable for the rest of his life. He was younger than but surely not as clever as I, Gray-Sin had smirked. No one talked about the rumors—rumors that Parry had taken his own life. Whether done quickly and with definite purpose or over time, via needles, pills, or liquor, Gray-Sin had no respect for the man. Turning on his heel once again, Gray-Sin walked away.

As he moved toward the opposite end of the room, there was an array of what appeared to be old-fashioned movie posters on a wall covered with heavy theater drapery. Each advertised what looked like an epic, big screen motion picture. There was the African woman, the young lady in her own blood on the city street, Miss Woodrie holding out a test paper with a disappointed look upon her face, and the movie poster of Sam Parry, who according to Gray-Sin, was a most pathetic specimen of a human being. Each was titled with a quotation.

Below the mother who had lost two of her beloved children, the lines stated, "Love your enemies and pray for those who persecute you …" (Matthew 5:44) How could a mother ever love the enemies who sicken, steal, and kill her children, contemplated Gray-Sin in disgust.

Next to the desecrated young woman left alone on the street, "Even though I walk through the valley of the shadow of death, I fear no evil; for you are with me …" (Psalm 23:4)

"But … how?" Gray-Sin cleared his throat and signed, "She didn't deserve that."

Above the image of Parry, "… if your brother sins, rebuke him, and if he repents, forgive him; and if he sins against you seven times in the day, and turns to you seven times, and says, 'I repent,' you must forgive him." (Luke 17:3-4)

"Interesting," Gray-Sin quietly decided aloud.

Upon closer inspection, there was a verse written on the exam paper in Miss Woodrie's delicate, thin hands, "A false balance is an abomination to the Lord, but a just weight is his delight." (Proverbs 11:1)

"Well, I certainly don't hold anything against the teacher or …" his voice trailed off.

There was one more poster. Gray-Sin wondered which movie in life it might illustrate. Shocked, he took a double-take, realizing it was an identical image of himself. Engraved across the top of the poster frame was the quotation, "For we shall all stand before the judgment seat of God …" (Romans 14:10)

Chapter Twelve

"Oh, no," Gray-Sin slowly said aloud. "I probably should have done some things differently. I wish there was an opportunity for some kind of second chance—what was it we referred to as kids? Oh, yes, a do-over. If I had another chance, I'd make a difference, this time."

The hawk was perched on the edge of Gray-Sin's own poster reproduction. "Would you?" questioned Lily, staring at Gray-Sin.

"Well," he hesitated, stroking his chin, "if I had the chance to—"

"—That can be arranged." She flew off, two large, heavy wings lifted her as she sang and ultimately echoed, "Lily, Lily, Lily …"

QUESTIONS AND REFLECTIONS:

How can the perception of guilt be a weakness and a strength? Does God lead you when you feel guilty? Reflect on this process, and share if you can.

Have you ever been able to "enter a scene" and change it or the outcome? Were the results expected? Did it allow for personal or spiritual growth? Have you ever walked away from that type of situation? Were you relieved, saddened, or left unsatisfied?

Part III
ILLUMINATION

CHAPTER
Thirteen

"Natural History" was the title above the double doors. Reaching for the large brass handle, Gray-Sin pulled one of the massive doors, opened it, and entered the room, surprised at the smoothness and ease with which it moved. He was tempted to look over his shoulder to make sure that neither the bird nor anyone or anything else had followed him. There were the predictable displays around the perimeter of the room, such as stuffed mammals from various regions of the world. In the center of the chamber, skeletal structures of great mammals that no longer roamed the earth were posed: Mastodons, Mammoths, Cave Bears, Saber Tooth Tigers, and Giant Sloths. Funny, Gray-Sin reflected, that he remembered the names. When his children were young, Gray-Sin would read to them at night. He would not waste time with silly bedtime stories. Rather, he taught his children about nature and the importance of history and learning from the past. Amusing thoughts permeated his imagination about something in the room eating that obnoxious hawk. He realized that it had been a long time since he allowed himself to daydream.

In the next corridor of the same wing, Gray-Sin recognized another one of his specialties—Botany. There was vegetation of various biomes from many time periods in numerous world regions. In the flowering plant section, Gray-Sin was drawn to a glass-covered, wooden-framed and cherry-stained case titled, "Historically Referenced Plants." It contained dried samples as well as drawings and sketches from well-documented journals of famous explorers. All were completely labeled. Some varieties were used medicinally, others for paints, make-up, and pigments, while a small sample were used as lethal poisons.

Gray-Sin read the note inside the glass-covered diorama about the beautiful white Easter lily, a symbol of purity, life, and the eternal newness of spring and rebirth. Below the description was an explanation:

> In the well-known Sermon on the Mount, Christ taught, 'Consider the lilies of the field, how they grow; they neither toil nor spin …' (Matthew 6:28) Church paintings often portray the Angel Gabriel holding and offering white lilies to the Virgin Mary, proclaiming that in her purity, she would conceive and bear the Messiah.

The shrill, high-pitched call of a hawk was heard. It was not the singing that Gray-Sin was growing accustomed to, and the word Annunciation reverberated through his mind. Was the hawk announcing anything of importance? What was the Annunciation really about in the stretch of time before the birth of the Christ Child? Gray-Sin remembered hearing the story at church each year during Advent, the season leading up to Christmas. Memories of his own mother emerged. She ensured that her children were dressed in their Sunday best as if that would somehow make the children behave and the stories easier to memorize. It was not that he was an unbeliever; it just didn't affect him, because it didn't seem to matter.

Gray-Sin was immersed in memories of his mother and suddenly found himself thinking about the Mother of Jesus. Had she been afraid? Gray-Sin remembered his childhood pastor remarking how history claimed that she was just a young teen. In the Gospel of Luke, Mary is quoted, "Behold, I am the handmaid of the Lord; let it be to me according to your word." The Bible verse is followed with, "And the angel departed from her." (Luke 1:38)

That, thought Gray-Sin, would have been frightening as well—to have gone through something of such magnitude and then, be left alone with whatever would happen next. Gray-Sin's thoughts trailed off as he wondered how or why that recollection even entered his mind. Then again, being left alone could have its merits too, he thought.

Walking past the next hallway, there were more paintings of plants and nature. He stopped in front of an expressive watercolor of a field. The meadow was partitioned by a weathered corral, old and abandoned, appearing to have been deserted for years. The fence line was low; perhaps smaller farm animals such as sheep or goats once occupied it. Most of the timeworn boards that were still standing, somehow stayed together. A gate, no longer held fast by hinges long ago rusted away, stood propped against a section of fencing. There was a horizontally-placed rectangular concrete block, a cover on top of what may have been an old well, sealing itself off from the surface of whatever was kept underground. A small brook ran along the exterior of the fence. As it wound around the pen, it worked its way back to a variety of deciduous trees. Gray-Sin was a city boy at heart, yet he still appreciated the outdoors. The trees grew within one hundred feet of the water and were then transposed into a variety of firs that climbed up a line of jagged rocks. He thought about the changing terrain made by layers of the Earth's surface that had been pushed up long ago. That created the taller, newer, and craggier mountains of western North America, unlike their older, lower, smoother, and rounder counterparts, the eastern hills of the United States, where erosion had taken its toll.

Gray-Sin focused on the small fenced area once again. Shepherds raised sheep. It was difficult work. Shepherds had to know each and every one of their flock. The sheep needed to be guided, fed, watered, protected from danger, returned when lost, and cared for during their entire lives. A shepherd didn't get to do much else. Not a high paying job, it was simply the job. He recalled having to memorize a Bible verse during Sunday school, "The good shepherd lays down his life for his sheep." (John 10:11) Gray-Sin remembered reading an article about Navajo women, who up until modern day, continue to be the shepherds of their families' sheep. Jesus was also the metaphorical shepherd, Gray-Sin gathered. It seemed that Jesus did not get much choice about who his flock would be.

Gray-Sin examined the picture for a moment longer. It brought a sense of comfort to him, maybe from a time long ago, when on his grandparents' farm. Perhaps there was something else, something more. He took a step forward to physically move on, but Gray-Sin found himself stepping back, back to the painting, yes, but also back to something he once had and once knew. He gazed at and admired the work, allowing it to stir a feeling of encouragement. Gray-Sin did not remember stepping away, and partially surprised yet acceptingly, found himself, once again in the subway tunnel.

QUESTIONS AND REFLECTIONS:

How have the first two subtitles (Part I – Arrival and Part II – Descent) affected Gray-Sin's journey? Does it suggest or lead you as a participant? What might Illumination refer to? Is there a concrete versus spiritual explanation or description? What could be required for illumination of one's mind, spirit, or soul?

In biblical days, what was the Annunciation? What was being announced? Did Mary, Mother of Jesus need the Annunciation? When, in her life, might Mary have been afraid? How do you respond to big announcements? What are your ideas about the symbols revealed in this chapter?

CHAPTER
Fourteen

The familiar subway background, lighting, and pungent smells permeated the senses. Gray-Sin felt surprisingly at home with the yellowed wall tiles, which seemed to prompt him to pick up the pace as he walked alongside the track. Once again, the cellist was a familiar form within the scene. He seemed to be marginally cleaned up. Gray-Sin looked upon the man's face. It was softer, as were his eyes. His voice was a rich baritone, no longer deep and raspy. "Welcome back, Gray-One. I am Simon Stone and hold your key." He reached out toward Gray-One, who hesitated to make contact with the gate-keeping musician. Instead of handing him anything though, Simon Stone raised an arm and pointed above the visitor's head. Gray-One turned around and looked up to view the place indicated by Stone.

"Who Trespass" was the phrase written across two tiles.

Sounds like a warning, Gray-One silently deliberated. "And what's with another name?" he muttered. He heard the train slowing to a stop, brakes squealing, as metal doors whined open. An old, bent man was standing next to him on the platform. He was apparently blind and held out an inverted baseball cap in one hand and cane in the other as he slowly walked, legs bowed.

"Pl ... pl ... please help," implored the aged man.

"How do I even know if you are truly blind?" accused Gray-One.

"Huh ... huh ... hun ... gry, sir."

Gray-One quickly stepped onto the train, and it sped into darkness. He found himself thinking and wondering how long the day had been. Outside, where there should have been windows to view from a train, a fog suddenly appeared, becoming thicker, denser, heavier. The coach raced onward, and the surroundings became darker and darker until all Gray-One could see were his thoughts. He contemplated his recent experiences. A Native American village that was so desecrated by Europeans and other immigrants, it was ironic that they would all later share the word American as part of their citizenship titles. He had seen children on that day, along with the beggar and Simon, the musician, with proclamations of a key. There were haunting memories of the African woman and her sorrows, but how could he have changed anything for her? Then, there was the reminder of Parry's wasted life, the cross in the wedding chapel, memories of Mama, whose life had been too short, his beloved wife, Faith, Grandmother, the crumpled woman on the street, and those hurtful school-age memories, all so real. The nagging Lily, Lily, Lily Hawk was becoming more and more of a comfort. At least she was often with him in his loneliness.

"Loneliness," he breathed. "I looked forward to solitude when this day arrived. Have I been lonesome today?" He ruminated about the difference between the two. Was the blind man really blind? Who was the true blind man?

"Would it have mattered whether or not he was blind?" a voice from nowhere and everywhere questioned.

"Hearing voices is one thing. Talking back to them is quite another," insisted Gray-One. "And while we're chatting, thanks for the new name. I actually like this one. I am, after all, older and certainly grayer than ever before. I'd like to think wisdom comes with the territory."

"Let's hope. Indeed, that would be purposeful," stated the voice. Gray-One could not tell if it was real or imagined. That should have concerned him, he decided.

Chapter Fourteen

The darkness seemed to completely envelope Gray-One, and the load became even more substantial. It was difficult for him to catch his breath, and he felt a crushing pressure all around his head, chest, and limbs. Gray-One, for the first time since he was a child, was frightened. The feeling became fuller and darker. It closed in on him and was overwhelming. All the while, there were visions, new and old, where his life had gone wrong and small inklings of what had been right. Where could he have made better choices? There were old hurts and fears. He suddenly saw his life as if through a magnifying glass. So much was about power and wealth. So much of his existence had been built upon one tally mark after another. Where did it get him? Had he lived a life full of contentment? What could have made him more joyful? He knew not the answer. He was not even sure what happiness was or what it felt like.

"Have you ever been hungry, tired, blind?" sweetly wheedled the voice of the perplexing, yet unseen bird.

"Why do you harass me, Hawk? I just want to have some happiness on this day—or even just a bit of peace! The child called you angel-hawk; you are certainly not my angel! Are you?"

"What do you say?" she proposed as her voice faded away.

"Angel or not, I want to be happy, but I wouldn't even recognize it if I had it!" he shouted, surprising himself with the outburst.

The train wheeled to an abrupt halt. Gray-One was thrown forward and landed on his hands and knees. "Please," he softly pleaded, "just show me the way."

QUESTIONS AND REFLECTIONS:

Who do you think Simon Stone represents to Gray-One as well as to others? Discuss the repeated reference related to the key and "Who Trespass." What is blindness?

Reread this chapter aloud with a partner or in a group. Note a word, phrase, or section that stands out to you. Can you see yourself in that passage or within the character now called Gray-One? Why has his name been changed again?

CHAPTER
Fifteen

"This is the way, walk in it …" (Isaiah 30:21) "I am the way, and the truth, and the life; no one comes to the Father, but by me." (John 14:6)

Still on his knees, Gray-One gripped a chair and pulled himself up. He had been there before. Everything was exactly the same, except that he was farther away from the altar at the front of the chapel, which was situated just before the ominous cross. From his vantage point, Gray-One could not see any higher than what must have been the bottom one-fourth of the wooden torture device. He approached and stood at the forefront of the room as if for the very first time. He could not have missed the forms at the base of the ill-intentioned tree. Only their backs were visible but cloaked. They were both kneeling. By the breadth of the shoulders, it was clear that one was a male and the other, a female.

The frailty of the woman could be detected in her cries of anguish and pain. She looked small as the man drew her to him, his arm around her shoulders. She shook from the sobs, which tore into the depth of Gray-One's soul. He was not a man who enjoyed seeing a woman cry, yet in most cases, was certainly able to distance himself from the emotionality of such a scene. This was not to be one of those circumstances. The woman raised her arms upward. Perhaps, it was with a desire to reach for what was left of the man nailed to the wood or perhaps, she strained past him. Gray-One noted how her hands and arms trembled. However, it was in the quivering that her weakness dissipated and she was strengthened in prayer. She was forward and unafraid. She knows who's in charge here, Gray-One surmised. It mattered not to her that there would be armed guards around this Jesus, let alone that she was a woman who lived in a time when such behavior could mean her being stoned.[1]

Who was this woman, whose pain bore into Gray-One? And then, he knew. Acknowledgment coincided with the moment he heard the narration from the topmost portion of the cross, "'Woman, behold, your son!' Then he said to the disciple, 'Behold your mother!' And from that hour the disciple took her to his own home." (John 19:26-27) And Gray-One looked upon the Mother of God. She was also the mother of his family, friends, and enemies. She was known as Myriam in ancient Hebrew and possibly Mariam in the spoken dialect of Aramaic. She was Mary from Nazareth, the small town in the city of Galilee, and had been betrothed to the local carpenter, Joseph. She was daughter of Anna and Joachim, the Immaculate Conception born in the absence of original sin, and Virgin Mother of Jesus the Christ.

What struck Gray-One was not her earthly frailty but a strength that came from elsewhere. She wailed and rocked as the beaten and lifeless, bloodied body was taken down and rested on her lap, the same lap where the child Jesus undoubtedly climbed into for comfort. She must have told him stories while on that very lap and possibly even heard his fears about friends and school and what would become of him. This Mary, Mother of Jesus, was not a painted icon of some fourth or fifth century monk but a real woman, his mother. As she cradled her dead son, her cries pierced Gray-One's heart. How could they have done this to another human being, let alone to *this* Man? What did he do that so angered the authorities and the mobs? Gray-One heard Mary whispering as her moans were subdued

---

[1] Edward Fronske, O.F.M., St. Francis Church, Whiteriver, AZ, theme from talks and retreats, 1998 – 2014

by breathlessness. She knelt, cradling her son's blood-stained head, the same head whose baby fine hair she once playfully tousled; his shoulders, the same that carried water for his loving mother and wood for his earthly father; and his arms, the same that were held out to his mother as he waited for a hug as a boy and the same that enveloped her as he entered manhood and must have assured her that God had a purpose for him.

Gray-One dared to step nearer and strained to hear the woman, "I want to forgive them, Lord. I must forgive them, Lord. Please help me to forgive them, my Lord," she whispered in broken breaths. Did he actually perceive those words? He had never read about or heard them from scripture, but in permitting himself to be immersed and drowned in the expression on her face, he was sure that was what Mary was saying.

Only a short time before, she had heard her son utter the words, "Father, forgive them; for they know not what they do." (Luke 23:34) This did not make forgiveness easy for his mother; it only made it possible. Even though Mary was present through much of the cruel torture, torment, agony, and Death, she could not sin. Gray-One wondered how much liberty we as humans have to forgive. After all, if this Jesus indeed suffered for all of mankind, what would it take to forgive each other? How could we possibly forgive the hurts, the sorrows, and those who cause us to suffer?

Going to church with his own mother had been something Gray-One and his siblings did. It was expected but seemingly lost its purpose and application when she was taken from them. Why didn't he ever see, feel, or experience what he was now being exposed to? Jesus and his family were real, not just names associated with events and stories as if a series of folktales in the bible. They were as real as his own family had been—maybe more so.

Gray-One was standing, once again, pushed to the rear of the space, staring at the base of the cross. The two figures were no longer there. He felt alone. At least others were with him just a short time ago. He found himself thinking back to a time in church with Mama. Gray-One remembered a rare occasion when both parents stood together in church. It was at the baptism of his baby brother, Thomas. Gray-One thought, maybe for the first time, about his own baptism. It had not been his choice; he was too young. Had it mattered? Would it matter, now?

From his vantage point, he glanced up toward the altar and base of the cross. Only the blood-stained and bruised feet of the crucified one could be seen suspended between Heaven and Earth. Gray-One gasped out loud as he saw Jesus, very much alive and standing on the ground at the bottom of the cross. Nonetheless, bloodied feet were still nailed to the wood. That made absolutely no sense to Gray-One. Jesus, himself, also stood at the base of the cross holding a mallet, fashioned of wood and stone. Jesus began nailing something to it, then turned to Gray-One and then back to the base of his own execution device. Small wooden plaques were being fixed to the wood by Jesus. He was a strong man, not the image many see of a broken figure, the symbol on many crucifixes. Gray-One stepped forward to read the small placards but was careful not to get too close. The first read, "… you were buried with him in baptism *[then, the sound of hammer pounding]*, in which you were also raised with him through faith in the working of God, who raised him from the dead." *[more hammer pounding as another sign was attached]* "… God made alive together with him, having forgiven us all our trespasses, having canceled the bond which stood against us with its legal demands *[hammer pounds]*; … this, he set aside, nailing it to the cross." *[one more pound]* (Colossians 2:12-14) Gray-One, with head bent, knelt.

QUESTIONS AND REFLECTIONS:

Who is the woman in front of the cross? Discuss her fear and lack of fear. What are the markers for the way you process any situation as fearful or confident?

Does this Jesus fit your description of Jesus? What message or sin would Jesus nail to the cross for you? How is the setting appropriate for a wedding and funeral all at the same time?

CHAPTER
Sixteen

Kneeling, Gray-One looked down at the marble-tiled floor and then upward. From his vantage point, he hadn't noticed that the area contained an ornate, overhead glass dome. It reminded him of the Capitol Building in Washington, D.C., but the ceiling was made of intricate glass panels and panes. His eyes swept the room for the crucifix. It was gone. Actually, he was gone, no longer in the chapel. Instead, he somehow found himself within a colossal, vaulted, and rounded room.

People! There were people everywhere. They were not simply milling about but moved with purpose. As they swept around Gray-One, it was as if he was either invisible or too unimportant to capture their attention. He realized he was still in a kneeling position, yet that did not seem to draw a response from anyone. As he pulled himself upright, Gray-One began to feel more isolated than ever before. He walked slowly and observed that this was some kind of central station, for he stood within the interior hub of what could be likened to equidistant spokes of a large wheel. Each rod or spindle could be followed from the middle of the room into separate shafts. Peering into the surrounding tunnels, Gray-One noted that each contained the familiar railroad tracks.

Chapter Sixteen

He craned his neck skyward to take in the superimposed fixture above this central pivotal point. A large, brilliant, and golden archaic scale hovered above the epicenter of the room, suspended by nothing that Gray-One could see. It was unbalanced, and one of the dishes was low so the other was high, although no mass could be observed on either plate. The asymmetry of the massive device concerned Gray-One. He looked around the room and then back up at the tipped scales. Glancing toward the level of the tracks nestled within each tunnel, his eyes instantly met a set of clear blue-grey eyes, set within the jovial face of an elderly lady. As he stared at her, he was sure he knew the woman, and then she spoke.

"One cannot cheat justice; the scales must be reset."

"Miss Woodrie!" Gray-One exclaimed.

"Yes, young man," she declared with familiarity and at the same time, authority. Miss Woodrie, now aged, yet with beautiful wrinkle-free skin, spoke in a voice as young as he remembered. "It's time to board," she assured Gray-One.

Before heading toward a path, one he was now sure he must travel, Gray-One glanced up and noted a simple hand-carved wooden sign, "Against Us."

He found himself systematically responding, "Yes, ma'am," as he turned toward the destined train tunnels, hearing the familiar sound of the doors opening, followed by the clanging metallic squeal of them closing, and then the sensation of jostling motion. Miss Woodrie's presence was no longer evident. Gray-One found himself looking around and wishing his teacher of long ago had been commissioned to accompany him. He could not recall such a sensation of intense, deep isolation.

On this particular subway journey, Gray-One stared out of what could have been the train's window. For the first time, while riding this subway line, he was able to view scenery. It was desolate and rocky. Gray-One was reminded of the eerie moonscape photos he had viewed from the early space era. It looked as though rain hadn't touched the dry, sandy environment in years.

The train slowed to a halt, less abruptly than the last time. Gray-One disembarked as if he had no say in the matter. He was standing among the rocks and sand and began the next part of his journey. He walked and walked, thinking he should tire and become hungry and thirsty. That did not occur, however Gray-One hungered for companionship and thirsted for purpose to this trip.

As he journeyed by foot, the sun became a driving, beating source of discomfort. Gray-One sensed that he was walking into a valley, descending farther into the hot, dry desert. There were no real plants to speak of, although dried strands of straw-like grasses lined the path he moved along. With each step, images crowded his mind: the African woman who lost two children, the Native American tribes robbed of their natural surroundings, the children who bullied him, his father, his brother and sister, who for all intents and purposes, were dead to him. Gray-One stewed about Sam Parry as well as the women in his life, the cheating and lust. What about his own children and their lives he knew so little of? The woman in the street … the business deals he made without regard to others and their lives … Faith, Mama, Grandmother … the blind beggar, Simon Stone, Lily Hawk … the cross, the nailed Man, so desecrated he was unrecognizable (Job 25:6; Psalm 22: 6-7) … and Blessed Mother, our Blessed Mother, how she suffered … oh, the pain that swept through his soul. Is suffering all there is, he grieved?

While journeying, Gray-One heard rustling sounds. At times, they followed him; at other times, they moved with him; and still, there were times when the noises raced ahead of him, no matter where he tried to turn. There was also an intense driving wind, so scorching, he could have been inside a convection oven with the fan blowing the 350-degree cooking heat evenly about him. He could feel the dial being turned up to four hundred, four-fifty, five hundred; he heard screams that became louder and louder. His head and ears were about to explode. He fell again, hearing a voice proclaim, "… for a righteous man falls seven times, and rises again; but the wicked are overthrown by calamity." (Proverbs 24:16)

Chapter Sixteen

The heat and the agonizing cries of suffering permeated the depths of Gray-One, suffocating his existence and blotting out the man he had been. Where could he find help? Who would come to his aid? The shrieks, moans, and breathless grunts terrified him, causing further lamentation. Then, he recognized the voice of the cries as his own.

There was a great rushing sound. Was it wind or maybe a tornado? This could be an earthquake, Gray-One thought as he struggled to his feet and the surface beneath him rumbled. He wondered whether he had suffered second or third-degree burns. How would he manage to stand up and endure? The force was too much to bear. A great circling, whirling font of water was originating as a spring at his own feet. It was filling up the valley as far as he could see, as if a draining tub was video recorded and replayed in reverse. It was cold, frothy, and dark, moving rapidly with a hard odor. His knees were covered, then his waist, and upon reaching his mouth, tasted saltier than any ocean he had ever experienced. Gray-One had been a strong swimmer as an adult. He fought to keep his head above the chop. It was so vast and so lonely. He was insignificantly small. The sky was a mass of dark, low, wet, and chilling cold, swirling clouds, almost touching him, pushing downward. This is how it ends, he thought. He was going to drown. The intense pressure was now driving him under, deeper and deeper, closer to what must be the bottom. It seemed endless. Breathing was impossible. Holding his breath was impossible. Life was impossible. Finality was unavoidable … darkness, loneliness, and so much pressure.

Gray-One wondered … when would his life pass before him? Would he meet his Maker? He was scared, sad, and remorseful; he felt as wretched as one could. To revile himself was not enough. He was somehow in the midst of what could only be his own death, incomprehensibly separated from the vast external source of life itself.

And then, in an instant, he was overtaken by searing cold. An icy and barren landscape was all around. He looked about and shook his head in disbelief as he tried to focus his blurred vision. Could it be? Gray-One seemed to be atop a mountain, so far removed from civilization that he could see nothing but ice and snow. Clouds once again encircled him. They were thin and wispy; the fog closed in. Albeit astounded that he was suddenly dressed for sub-zero conditions and in fact, dry, nothing he ever felt was as cold and icy as he was now. The air was thin and barely detectable as Gray-One gasped for oxygen. It was as if he endeavored to breathe through the smallest drink stirrer. As his breathing diminished, becoming fainter, Gray-One realized that he was sprawled upon the snow and ice. Each attempt to draw in breath was worse than the previous one. His throat burned with the cold, lungs refusing to comply and inflate; particles of ice forced closed eyelids, nostrils, and lips. If I had … but one … chance … left … sorry … so, so … sor … Gray-One's thoughts clouded and trailed off as he perceived the likeness of a large and merciful hand reaching toward him.

QUESTIONS AND REFLECTIONS:

Why is it important for Miss Woodrie and Gray-One to reunite? Discuss the relevance of the over-sized scales.

Gray-One journeys again, and he meets up with great forces of nature. As he is about to lose consciousness or perhaps his own existence, there is the perception of a large, merciful hand reaching toward him. How is this chapter significant for Gray-One, yourself, or someone you are close to?

CHAPTER
Seventeen

"The steps of a man are from the Lord, and he establishes him in whose way he delights; though he fall, he shall not be cast headlong, for the Lord is the stay of his hand." (Psalm 37:23-24)

"Please Lord," Gray-One sobbed, "Please … what is it you ask of me?" The discomfort and pain were instantly gone.

"Arise, my son." Gray-One identified the same voice from earlier.

Gray-One stood up, surprised that he could do so. He looked down at himself. There were no burns, no salty waves, no ice. He was no longer covered with the heavy outerwear. "Thank you," he whispered, "thank you." Looking around, there were so many trails from which to choose. Still whispering, "How do I know the way to go?"

"The true path is narrow but illuminated by me, the Messiah, even in the darkness."

He felt the wake of the feathers before he saw her. His Lily Hawk flew past the left side of his head and passing on a steep angle toward him, moved in front of Gray-One, circling the right side of his face. As she performed her aerial maneuver, their eyes locked, and in that brief encounter, he heard her maternal voice in his heart. "I have been sent to guide you unto the truth; continue onward," and she was gone as quickly as she had appeared.

Chapter Seventeen

As Gray-One walked, he left the desert vale. He ascended first, onto a rocky hillside covered with wisps of short, scrubby plants and then to green pastures. The breeze was as refreshing as a cool drink. Gray-One continued to climb until he found himself upon a path. He walked along, enjoying the view and bird songs. He could clearly see that the trail led to a stone building. Approaching an arched opening, Gray-One stepped inside. There was a track running alongside his course. He followed it until he noticed a break in the rails that formed a Y and continued into two separate tunnels.

Something on the ground, just past one side of the footpath's deviation, stopped Gray-One where he was. Now would be the time to turn toward or away from the shape. Gray-One continued in the direction of what was undoubtedly a human. As he drew nearer, his focus on the form became more distinct. "I wonder what has happened?" he whispered, as if hoping no one else could hear his voice.

Gray-One approached the man, who was lying on his side, and tried to assess whether there had been a railway accident or if this was the victim of a brutal beating. The disheveled man was unconscious, and Gray-One could just as easily have left. Instead, he knelt and felt for a pulse while he looked for signs of breathing. The first was faint and rapid, the second, weak and shallow. He tried to gently shake and awaken the poor man. When there was no response, Gray-One called out for help. He shouted as loudly as he could. No help arrived, but the man was roused. Gray-One bent down, his own face close to the one bruised and bloodied, and again tried to make contact. Gray-One applied pressure to the wounds and used his own necktie and handkerchief to bind the lacerations and stop the bleeding.

The distant and unmistakable sound of a train approaching instantly signaled Gray-One to bolt into further action. From his kneeling position, Gray-One cradled the man in his arms, and with strength he hadn't felt since in the prime of his adulthood, lifted the victim who had been entrusted to his care. As Gray-One stood up, he perceived the train's arrival. Still holding the semi-conscious man, Gray-One stepped forward. The sound of closing doors only preceded the jolting motion by seconds.

As if in an actual city, names of destinations appeared before him, above where the door of the subway car should have been. The movement of the train slowed to a gentle stop. Gray-One was surprised at how effortlessly he held the wounded, grown man in his arms. Upon the forward motion that propelled him outside the train, he noticed a sign with the word "Inn" etched in the yellow tiles. Walking along the platform, he reached an escalator and stepped up onto it. At the top, Gray-One continued to see signs to "Inn" and followed them. As if he was expected, double glass doors in front of them opened. An attendant appeared and silently motioned Gray-One to transfer the man to a wheelchair that he pushed. The man nodded at Gray-One and began wheeling the patient away.

"Wait," said Gray-One. The attendant looked back but then continued with the injured man. "Please wait." The wheel chair stopped; the orderly looked back. Reaching into his pocket, Gray-One started, "I will pay for this poor man's care," but realized once again, that his pockets were empty. "I must have left my wallet behind, but I will come back to pay for what is owed."

"You already have," acknowledged the caretaker.

Gray-One instantly recognized the man, "Simon Stone! Please—will this man be all right? Why have I been shown so many people of this place?"

"The key, Gray-One, remember the key. They have all been able to forgive. Have you?"

Stone walked off, pushing the wheelchair as if exiting the stage in a play.

QUESTIONS AND REFLECTIONS:

Apart from the obvious change in Gray-One's sense of compassion, what else is changing within the character? Do you feel, at this time in Gray-One's existence, that he would offer assistance to Sam Parry? Would you be capable of helping the Sam Parry in your life? How does Sam represent Gray-One's isolation?

Why is Simon Stone the attendant for the injured man? Whose voice was heard before Lily appeared again? How does Lily Hawk's return relate to Gray-One as well as the reader journeying through this study? What significance does the key continue to have?

Part IV
GLORY

CHAPTER
Eighteen

Returning to the escalator, Gray-One followed the signs to "Station." For as many times as he had ridden this transit system of passage, he had never before noticed so many informational symbols. As Gray-One stepped off the moving staircase into the familiar central area, the boundaries became blurred, as if underwater or viewed by someone without their eyeglasses. His crisp focal point was a vertical beam, set in the center of the colossal room. Gray-One approached. As he neared, the image was unmistakable. It was the crucifix and a human, each form distinct and separate.

"Jesus?" Gray-One inquired with the curiosity of a child.

At once, the timbers were pushed to the background and the Son of Man, radiant and risen, was standing so close that if Gray-One extended his own arms, they would have touched those that had been fixed to the cross beam. Once again, Gray-One was impressed by the physical stature and strength of the Christ. Their eyes met. Gray-One had never felt such warmth and familiarity. Instantly, he saw much of his past, both good and bad, as if watching a movie. Shame, happiness, sadness, and relief were some of the emotions he felt flooding into and out of his being all at the same time. The feelings could not be contained, nor did Gray-One wish them to be. The catharsis was overwhelming and satisfying, even when the memories were less than positive. This is what he came here for. Yes, he was sure. Gray-One suddenly knew God. He could hear him, speak with him, and know the love God freely gave from his infinitely divine heart.

Then, Jesus spoke, "Your road has not been easy, but it has been one of choice. In life, you are given many opportunities. How do you feel you have chosen?"

Gray-One could only be truthful to his Brother in Spirit. "Sometimes well and at other times …" his voice trailed off "… I have always done what I felt would benefit me, with little regard for anyone else. I am prepared for what happens now, because I know you are fair."

"You were paid during your lifetime, were you not?"

"Yes, Lord."

"Think of the man you helped at the last stop," reminded Jesus. "How did that make you feel?"

"Right," stated Gray-One. "It just felt right."

"As it should," responded Jesus. "Take all the darkness and make it right."

"Why should I deserve a prize at this time of my existence? What about those who've made the right choices all along?" questioned Gray-One.

"The vineyard belongs to the Father. He is as generous to those who accept his invitation to work at dawn, as to those who work in the last hour of the day." (Matthew 20:1-16) "Let us sit." They were immediately on the shore of a sea with ancient fishing boats casting and drawing their nets in the distance. The two came to a palm tree and sat together beneath the shade. The air was clean with a mild breeze. "Do you know the account of Abraham speaking with the Lord about the great sins of Sodom and Gomorrah?" Gray-One nodded, remembering the story from his childhood Sunday school classes. "Abraham was concerned about the innocent being swept away with the guilty. The Father assured him that if there were fifty innocent people, he would save the city. Abraham inquired about God's decision if only forty-five righteous existed, then forty, and so on down to ten blameless people. Abraham was guaranteed that destruction would indeed be avoided. (Genesis 18:20-32) I can promise you the very same, here and now."

Chapter Eighteen

Gray-One asked, "What if someone had come to my door in the middle of the night, asking for help, and my family was already asleep? I might have conveniently rolled over to go back to sleep. I might still make the wrong choice out of selfishness."

Jesus displayed patience, "If you do not get up to serve your visitor out of friendship, then surely you would do it because of his persistence." (Luke 11:5-8)

Gray-One simply stated, "Yes."

Jesus continued, "And I tell you, ask and you will receive, seek and you will find; knock and the door will be opened to you." (Luke 11: 9-10; Matthew 7:7)

"I am not sure that this pertains to me," interjected Gray-One, surprised by his own level of comfort in speaking with Jesus. "There have been no gifts during my lifetime, only determination and hard work. I've never obtained anything for free. Yet, my heart feels the burden of insurmountable debt."

"The debt has already been paid; the Cross was once and for all. Our Father in heaven loves us too much to give us everything we ask for," reassured Jesus.[2]

"What does that really mean?" insisted Gray-One.

"The Father knows what his children need," said Jesus, smiling. "What father among you, if his son asks for a fish, will instead of a fish give him a serpent …?" (Luke 11:11) "If you then, who are evil, know how to give good gifts to your children, how much more will your Father who is in heaven give good things to those who ask him!" (Matthew 7:11)

"Lord, even I, a sinner many times over, do love my children." Gray-One instantly saw a series of reflections of his two daughters, from youth through adulthood. A strong desire to know the women better and spend more time with them overwhelmed him. He wished to reach out and hold each one but was unable to realize that desire. The longing was overbearing.

"Loved ones have prayed for you to have peace."

---

[2] Edward Fronske, O.F.M., retreats and homilies, St. Francis Church, Whiteriver, AZ, 1996 – 2014.

Gray-One lowered his gaze. "Lord," he slowly cried, "with all due respect, and please be patient with me, but why is it you speak to me now, after my whole life?"

"Son, I have always spoken to you. There were times, long ago, that you almost heard; you thought you heard. It is still not too late."

"So many temptations chronicled my lifetime," started Gray-One. "Why do you still offer me so much, even when I did not choose you?"

Jesus spoke, making direct and loving eye contact, "Because I have always chosen you."

Gray-One, suddenly full of love and yearning, turned toward Jesus and sinking from a standing to kneeling position, pleaded, quietly sobbing, "Please, teach me to pray."

Jesus responded, just as he did to his disciples, "When you pray, say:

> Father, hallowed be your name. Your kingdom come. Give us each day our daily bread; and forgive us our sins, for we ourselves forgive every one who is indebted to us; and lead us not into temptation." (Luke 11:2-4)

Closing his eyes, Gray-One repeated, word by word, line by line. When he opened them, Gray-One was again in the station. He could not see Jesus but was sure of his presence. Looking upward toward the crystal dome, he saw only the cross. This time, it was empty. There was no corpse, no Holy Mother or lone disciple. There was only a shining, white linen banner with violet letters and a brilliant golden trim, formed in elegant calligraphy and draped across the horizontal beam, resting against the stem of its vertical counterpart. On it, a bold and definitive statement proclaimed, "He himself bore our sins in his body on the tree, that we might die to sin and live to righteousness. By his wounds you have been healed." (1 Peter 2:24; Isaiah 53:5)

Gray-One, still on his knees, understood the depth of the declaration. "I have been healed," he breathlessly stated, repeating the unbelievable and self-judged undeserved truth, over and over again. Hearing a sound from above, Gray-One looked toward the ceiling. One white dove emerged, flying in a vertical, spiraling pattern and continued skyward, until it exited through the glass dome. As the dove soared up and out of the highest point, which suddenly became windowless, the golden, suspended Scales of Justice righted themselves, becoming rebalanced as the man allowed himself to forgive and to be forgiven.

A saturating light, warmer and brighter than any Gray-One had ever experienced or could have imagined, drew him in and became a part of his own essence. Looking down at himself, arms extended outward, the cufflinks, suit, and tie were gone. He was bathed in the rays and was so humbled and joyful that tears spilled from his eyes. He heard a sound so beautiful that it could not be described or compared to anything he had ever experienced in life. As the being moved effortlessly, enveloped by light and love, he saw Jesus, his friend and the physical embodiment of the Spirit of his Father God.

Embracing what was left of the man born into the world as Grayson, Jesus smiled, "Grace-Son, rejoice because your name is written in heaven." (Luke 10:20) And the spirit and soul of the redeemed followed the Savior into eternity.

QUESTIONS AND REFLECTIONS:

Jot down notes, ideas, and images from this final section, "Glory." How is Grace-Son's passage your journey? How may it change your journey? Discuss, if possible.

What thoughts and emotions do you have after reading Grace-Son's allegorical and experiential examination to ultimate and eternal purification?

BIBLIOGRAPHY

Edward Fronske, O.F.M. (Director) Talks. *Retreats and Homilies*. Conducted from St. Francis Church, Whiteriver, AZ, 1996 – 2019

www.ingramcontent.com/pod-product-compliance
Ingram Content Group UK Ltd.
Pitfield, Milton Keynes, MK11 3LW, UK
UKHW022223230426
12048UKWH00016BA/1023